WHO?

Ellen Raskin

Weekly Reader Children's Book Club presents

WHO, SAID SUE, **SAID WHOO**?

ATHENEUM, NEW YORK, 1973

Copyright © 1973 by Ellen Raskin
All rights reserved
Library of Congress catalog card number 72-86947
ISBN 0-689-30096-4
Published simultaneously in Canada by
McClelland & Stewart, Ltd.
Manufactured in the United States of America
Printed by Connecticut Printers, Inc., Hartford, Connecticut
Bound by A. Horowitz & Son/Bookbinders, Clifton, New Jersey
First Printing February 1973
Second Printing October 1973
Weekly Reader Children's Book Club Edition

FOR JEAN KARL
AND DAVID ROGERS
WITH MANY, MANY THANKS,
AND FOR SUZANNE GLAZER, TOO.
WHO?
SUE.

Who said moo?

The polka dot cow said moo.
 Then who, said Sue,
 Said chitter-chitter-chatter,
 And who said whoo?

MOO

WHOO

The cross-eyed owl said whoo,
The polka dot cow said moo;
    Then who, said Sue,
    Said chitter-chitter-chatter,
    And titter-tatter, too?

TITTER-TATTER

Titter-tatter, said the shrew.
The cross-eyed owl said whoo,
The polka dot cow said moo;
    Then who, said Sue,
      Said chitter-chitter-chatter,
      And quitter-quatter, too?

The goose said quitter-quatter;
Titter-tatter, said the shrew.
The cross-eyed owl said whoo,
The polka dot cow said moo;
    Then who, said Sue,
    Said chitter-chitter-chatter,
    And what's a roo?

The kangaroo's a roo.
The goose said quitter-quatter;
Titter-tatter, said the shrew.
The cross-eyed owl said whoo,
The polka dot cow said moo;
    Then who, said Sue,
    Said chitter-chitter-chatter,
    And who said boo?

I'M A ROO.

The billy goat's ghost said boo!
The kangaroo's a roo.
The goose said quitter-quatter;
Titter-tatter, said the shrew.
The cross-eyed owl said whoo,
The polka dot cow said moo;
    Then who, said Sue,
    Said chitter-chitter-chatter,
    And gnitter-gnatter, too?

Gnitter-gnatter, said the gnu.
The billy goat's ghost said boo!
The kangaroo's a roo.
The goose said quitter-quatter;
Titter-tatter, said the shrew.
The cross-eyed owl said whoo,
The polka dot cow said moo;
    Then who, said Sue,
    Said chitter-chitter-chatter,
    And spitter-spatter, too?

GNITTER-GNATTER

Two pigs said spitter-spatter;
Gnitter-gnatter, said the gnu.
The billy goat's ghost said boo!
The kangaroo's a roo.
The goose said quitter-quatter;
Titter-tatter, said the shrew.
The cross-eyed owl said whoo,
The polka dot cow said moo;
    Then who, said Sue,
    Said chitter-chitter-chatter,
    And who said 'choo?

SPITTER-
SPATTER

The chimp has a cold: A-choo!
Two pigs said spitter-spatter;
Gnitter-gnatter, said the gnu.
The billy goat's ghost said boo!
The kangaroo's a roo.
The goose said quitter-quatter;
Titter-tatter, said the shrew.
The cross-eyed owl said whoo,
The polka dot cow said moo;
    Then who, said Sue,
    Said chitter-chitter-chatter,
    And who said shoo?

A-CHOO

The honeydew snake said shoo!
The chimp has a cold: A-choo!
Two pigs said spitter-spatter;
Gnitter-gnatter, said the gnu.
The billy goat's ghost said boo!
The kangaroo's a roo.
The goose said quitter-quatter;
Titter-tatter, said the shrew.
The cross-eyed owl said whoo,
The polka dot cow said moo;
    Then who, said Sue,
    Said chitter-chitter-chatter?
    WHO?

SHOO

Moral: **Words aren't everything.**